FRIENDS & LOVERS

by

NOEL LORENZ

NOEL LORENZ HOUSE OF FICTION

Title of Book: Friends & Lovers
Author of Book: Noel Lorenz
Series: World Literature Series, Book - 1
First Published in India in Feb. 2021 by Noel Lorenz House of Fiction
Editor: Abhisek Ghosh (Pen Name - Noel Lorenz)
Cover Design: Copyright © Abhisek Ghosh, 2020.
Copyright © Abhisek Ghosh, 2020.

ISBN 13: 978-81-950006-6-1
Noel Lorenz House of Fiction
Headquarters - Kolkata, West Bengal, India
154A, KCG Road, Kolkata - 700050
www.noellorenz.com

Dedicated

To Earth

PREFACE

This book is a dream come true. I have always dreamed to release an international book where writers from many countries have contributed.

Thanks to Katherine Abraham, the compiler and Brand Ambassador of NLHF for the World Literature Series, that my dream has come true at last, and I am sure, this is just the start.

The stories and poems in this book are special as thinkers and writers have come together to sprinkle their literary intelligence to make this book a wonderful read. I have added a paranormal micro-tale at the end to add spice to the already interesting book.

~

Noel Lorenz
10 Feb 2021
Kolkata, India

ACKNOWLEDGEMENTS

- I want to thank the Brand Ambassador. It was only with their help that I was able to compile this book.
- I want to thank all the writers from around the world.
- I want to thank my parents for all the time I was busy editing this book.
- I want to thank Goddess Saraswati for blessing me to be the editor of such a wonderful work of art.

BRAND AMBASSADOR

CONTENTS

UNAVOIDABLE LOVE

ALLISON WHITTENBERG

About the Author

▬

Allison Whittenberg is a Philadelphia native who has a global perspective. If she wasn't an author she'd be a private detective or a jazz singer. She loves reading about history and true crime. She loves horror movies and observational comedy. Her novels include Sweet Thang, Hollywood and Maine, Life is Fine, Tutored and The Sane Asylum.

What do you do in your leisure time?

dance, sing, read

from

Philadelphia, U.S.A.

Some people fall into love for recreation. It's simply something to do to pass the time and with summer and it's long, long days, romance proves the perfect time murderer as a rule these flings was supposed to end right about now just as August drifts into September. Maybe, I should look at things like that and just get back to school and prepared for cold weather. Of course, that was the catch for all those who fell in love extra curricularly -- falling out of love. It's never as easy as falling in. During this falling out, my world went black. Time moves differently. Loneliness unfolded. I was a prisoner, trying to dig my way out of this cell with a spoon that I pinched from the proverbial mess hall. When I was out earlier in the day with Mom, I realized the wind seemed freer, harsher. Already, fall was coming on strong. Okay, so it's only been a week since Reid left, but what a week and maybe I won't feel this way the rest of my life, but what if I did. What if I never get out of lockdown? At any rate, I took advantage of my me-time and made that kind of popcorn that's kind of salty and kind of sweet. I sat in front of the TV preparing myself for the distraction but on the first fistful, I had to put it in the side. The large digital clock on my desk flipped to 9:19 just as the doorbell pealed.

I stomped downstairs thinking whoever it was on the other side of the door better have a good reason for being there. "Who is it?" I asked, in a harsh bug off pest voice as I peeked through the peephole. I saw him, and I didn't wait for his answer. My shaking hands flung the door open. My eyes searched him, my head spinning. I felt dizzy, excited, and confused all at once. He smelled like fresh-cut grass. His eyes sparkled. His shoulders squared. "Lizzy, I just heard about what happened with Alexa. I'm so sorry." It was a warm night with tons of insects buzzing about. The porch light drew them to this area. "I'm guessing my mom called you." He nodded. "Believe me, that wasn't your fault, Reid. All I had to do was stay away like you said, and she wouldn't have ended up in the hospital." "She's a grown woman, you're not responsible for her." "If I called the police, she would have never attacked herself." "You saved her life." I frowned. "For how long?" "That's up to her... Your mom also said that you're readmitted to school." "Tomorrow." "I thought they would at least give you until after the holiday." "What's Labor Day mean to me? I'm not complaining. I've had enough of a break." "Well, I'm sure you'll have a great year," he said and turned to leave. That's when my fast beating heart stopped cold. "That's it?" I asked. "I just wanted to see that you were all right, Lizzy." I stepped out to the porch. "You were the one who told me if I was ever in a jam to call you." "Yeah, and you got in a jam, a big one, and you didn't." "You must know that I think of you all the time, Reid." He looked away. "I am sorry I brought Alexa into your life. I had no idea she was this -- " "I don't want to talk about Alexa.

Some other time maybe, but not now." He nodded, still keeping his distance. "I really better get going." "So let me get this straight." I now stood before him. "You came all the way over here not to visit." He didn't retreat he just repeated, "I just wanted to see if you're alright." "That's the only reason?" I asked leadingly. He kept a steady gaze on me. "Lizzy, why else would I come by?" "Well, you could have just missed me?" Just then, a moth lost itself to the flame. "Lizzy, that goes without saying." I shrugged. "Say it anyway." His smile was so warm, so easy, but he didn't utter a word. I was now close enough to him. My fingers tickled down his arm, and I finally blurted out, "Are you married yet, or are you still planning on waiting 26 years?" That made him laugh. I missed his laugh. Books go on and on about how true love has no end, but I never believed in. Absolutes are hard for me to wrap my mind around. But to be this close to him. To smell his smell and hear his voice and feel his skin there was something there. His hand came behind my neck, and he brought his lips down to mine, and I tilted my face up. I was all prepared to be furiously kissed by him, but then he pulled himself away, saying, "It's a school night." I sighed, cocked my head to the side, and told him, "Yeah, but I don't have homework yet." I crushed his lips beneath mine and pinned him against the banister. And I knew this was wrong. So wrong to lapse back into things. But that's all life is really a series of uneven moments who really cares what's right or wrong. In the future, a hundred years or a thousand years or maybe even a million short years from tonight, who's even going to know that a Reid Lansky or an Elizabeth "Lizzy" Mell existed?

Certainly, no one will care that he was 23 and I, only 18. A few seconds with him made me forget the present-day reality of things. It was like we never broke up. And I no longer felt quite lost and so sad. Right then, it was all about the still of the night, the stars, the half-moon, the saving off the inevitable.

BLISS

SAN LIN TUN

About the Author

San Lin Tun (b.1974) is a freelance writer of essays, poetry, short story and novel in Myanmar and English. He holds Dip in (BDh), B.E (Metallurgy), and M.A (BDh).

He was a first prize winner of poetry for 2015 Wales National Day. And, he has published thirteen books in English and his latest novel "An English Writer" came out in 2019.

His writings can be read in Asia Literary Review, Borderless, Countercurrent, Kitaab, Litehouse, Mad in Asia Pacific, Mekong Review, NAW, PIX, Ponder Savant, South East of Now and several others.

He is now working on his second novel.

What do you do in your leisure time?

I play guitar and sometimes draw cartoons.

from

Yangon, Myanmar

It was a dull and lethargic Sunday afternoon with clouds hanging low in the sky. At first, Su felt a bit drowsy because of heat and boredom. So, she went over to the window to open and to stream the air in as she felt suffocating.

She also tried to get rid of such torpor from her because she did not want to take a nap at this moment. Apart from looking at the rail track in front of her house, she had no other things to do. Then, Su switched her gaze to the bright sky and found the clouds as immobile as her.

Her mind started to drift away to the last train trip she was together with her husband when she heard a loud whistling of a 3:30 up-country train which would be roaring by her house in a few minutes.

A moment later, she saw some passengers gazing out from the windows although she saw them in a flash. She thought that some saw her standing by the window and looking at them. Suddenly, she smiled when she remembered that it was such a pleasurable trip they had made together, and they had a chance to redefine and amend their almost collapsed situation once more.

≈

And, during the trip, they nearly forgot about everything including their worries, their financial problems, and everything in this incredible trip. They enjoyed every moment of it. Her husband showed Su much warmth which she needed more than at home, and he became a real man again.

It was her husband's plan to take a train trip to a beach when he sensed that their marriage situation led to a bad and rocky state. Even he scolded Sue when she made a trivia mistake and when she cooked the same curry for two consecutive days. Sometimes, he came back home drinking with the reason of tiredness and fatigue. That time, she was bitterly frustrated with their marriage situation which had reached its five years of wedlock. She wondered whether they could get out of this difficult situation.

She prayed and prayed to overcome the dilemma. Su understood that at that time, he was nearly out of his job, and debts were nagging them. And, as for a housewife, she became restless. Upon one of their closest friend's suggestion, her husband thought they should take a trip to forget every miserable thing they had been facing in. After careful consideration, they decided to take a trip to a beach. They borrowed some money from their closest friends who sympathized with their difficult situation, letting them have the money they wanted for the journey. Later, the couple found that their plan went well, and it brought back every bit of drained energy that they needed for restoring their life back to strengthen their wedlock after the vacation for three days at the beach.

Sue still remembered that unbelievable sojourn whenever she heard a train coming. Suddenly, she was startled when someone gently touched her shoulder and abruptly interrupted her thought.

≈

She quickly turned around to see her husband, who held a bouquet in his hand. With a huge and warm smile, he extended his hand to her and said, "Happy Sixth Anniversary!!! Thank you very much for choosing me to be your man."
His voice was clear and sweet.
She looked at him affectionately and kissed him softly. Quickly her eyes were filled with joyful tears.

DEVORAH'S DEMISE

JENEAN MCBREARTY

About the Author

Chocolate. Tea. Hangin' out So.Cal. style. That's me. Even though I live in Kentucky, I'm a California kind'a gal. I collect college degrees ... I'm working on a 3rd MA because what do teachers do when they retire? They learn. I also collect pictures of soldiers, battles, and world leaders. I love history. Like they say, the only thing new in the world is the history you don't know. I wish I was young enough to qualify for the space force. I'd love to explore the universe.

What do you do in your leisure time?

Read, write, submit, reeat.

from

Danville, KY
U.S.A.

"I understand that you want to kill Shelby Connover, Devon, I just don't understand why." Deborah loved being half of "Devorah," but had seen the couples' relationship as Chalfont St. Giles' society darlings becoming clouded.

Devon was sitting in his wing-back before a lack-luster fire, surrounded by tissues he used to wipe each tear. After three outbursts of rage, he was a spent spigot of near estrogenic proportions. "You have a stiff upper lip. I must, to my own self be true," he said in his Lawrence Olivier voice.

Deborah wasn't there when the battle was joined. All she knew of the seismic canyon that now existed between Bristol's most notable bromance she heard from Shelby's wife, Mercedes. "It happened when Shelby turned toward the buffet table to get another cocktail, and accidentally stepped on Devon's foot. 'How dare you!' Devon shouted, and gave Shelby a slap that sent him reeling into the geraniums. The waiter stood him right, but Shelby's white jacket bore a mud scar. He belted Devon in satisfaction."

"Did Shelby apologize for the foot infraction?" Deborah had asked. She was never one to express an opinion when fact-finding. "Who knows? Devon let loose with a string of enthralling American expletives, cutting Shelby in half. Oh, Deborah, promise we won't let this incident between husbands jeopardize our friendship."

They pinky-swore. Deborah left the tea-shop as soon as propriety allowed and immediately went to the cobblers. "The scuff isn't permanent, is it?"

"I doubt it," the cobbler said, "they're Brooks Brother's finest alligator. At nineteen hundred American dollars a pair, they'll last through trench warfare."

That's when Deborah rushed home to deliver the cleaned shoes and good news and found Devon in despair, his captured 9 mm German luger laying in his lap. "Is this really about shoes?" she said.

"How would you feel if both you and Mercedes showed up at a party wearing a new dress? You ask how much she paid for it and she gets offended ..."

"Oh God, Devon, you didn't ask Shelby how much he paid for his new shoes!"

"Your damn right I did. He was wearing loafers from Harry's of London. The same twenty-two hundred-dollar shoes we saw last week. Then he says, 'Don't worry, ol' boy, no one will think you cheap.' Yes, my American-made shoes cost less, but I got a belt for five-hundred-dollars. That's twenty-five hundred dollars. But how are people to know that? I can't carry my belt like a purse."

Deborah's stiff upper lip quivered. Devon had acclimated to England, but his fashion aesthetic remained American. Divorce was inevitable. She called Mercedes but got no answer. Shelby had obviously put his foot down, voiding their pinky swear with patriarchic finality.

There was only one thing to be done. Yes, Americans preferred murder to suicide, which was obvious, too, as Devon had wept for hours and had yet to pull the trigger. If only he was German, he would have ended her misery outside under a Linden. If he was Russian, he might have thrown himself under a train. For the carpet's sake, there was consolation he wasn't Japanese else she'd have to call the cleaners before her book club met on Thursday next.

When she lowered her head in mourning for past friendships, Deborah's eyes could not avoid staring at the intricate pattern the Persians had woven into the rug. Her head drooped a smidgen more when she noticed a small patch that seemed threadbare. Not unusual for antiques, she told herself, but still … perhaps she could persuade Shelby to let Mercedes help her shop for a replacement. Yes, that's what she needed. A replacement. She would ring Shelby in the morning.

"Give me your pistol, Devon, I have to tidy up before dinner," she said before taking aim at his lovely Ohioan skull. When disgrace is the entrée, it is best to dine alone.

POSSIBILITY

B.A. BRITTINGHAM

About the Author

The author, formerly of New York City and South Florida, is currently a resident of Southwestern Michigan, and has published essays in the Hartford Courant; short stories in Florida Literary Foundation's hardcover anthology, Paradise; with the University of Georgia Center for Continuing Education; in the 1996 Florida First Coast Writers' Festival and in Britain's World Wide Writers. "The Note in the Wood," was a semi-finalist in the 2003 Nelson Algren Awards and was published in the June 2008 issue of Shore Magazine. "Loose Ends" was published in Storyteller-Short Fiction. She is also a photographer.

from

Three Oaks, Michigan U.S.A.

There is a portion in each of us that will never know why something did or did not happen; such things have a way of sticking with us like a tiny, persistent splinter on the knuckle, or an after-dark toothache. What became of that handsome lad who on a long ago Saturday evening (was I ever really twenty?) so smoothly, so surreptitiously seduced me, and even as I knew what was happening, refused to stop it, instead resolutely telling myself, 'Quit thinking everything to death!' All factors were in the way: paired spouses, distance, futures, vocations, and yes, even morality. From the other side of forty years, knowing well that it could have turned out badly in so many variations, still, it is thought of in an affable amber luminosity. There was a beginning but no definitive ending. There never will be except in the grand universe of once-here-now-lost possibility; and perhaps that is the finest result, the endless alternatives of maybe.

- STAY

- FLASHBACK

- STARLIGHT CONFESSION

KELLI J. GAVIN

About the Author

Kelli J Gavin of Carver, Minnesota is a Writer, Editor, Blogger and Professional Organizer. Her work can be found with Clarendon House Publishing, Sweetycat Press, The Ugly Writers, Sweatpants & Coffee, Zombie Pirates Publishing, Setu, 300 South Media Group, Cut 19, Otherwise Engaged, Flora Fiction, Love What Matters, Printed Words and Southwest Media among others. Kelli's first two books were released in 2019 ("I Regret Nothing- A Collection of Poetry and Prose" and "My Name is Zach- A Teenage Perspective on Autism"). She has also co-authored 18 anthology books. With two more books to be released in 2021, she is also working on a collection of fiction short stories.

Her blog can be found at www.kellijgavin.blogspot.com .

@KelliJGavin on Twitter, Instagram and Facebook

What do you do in your leisure time?

Swim, watch movies, nature walks spend time with friends and family

STAY

from

Please stay

Closer

Even closer

When you walk away

Sometimes even when you run

I wonder and wait for you to return

The physical separation hurts

Questioning if you will come back

Praying that you will

If I give you enough time

You are usually restored to me

I have found your presence is essential

For me to continue functioning

Please remain

Please stay

Always within reach

FLASHBACK

It takes only one sight

One sound

Even a scent

And I am brought back

To a time when things were easy

I flashback to when things were smooth

Time seemed to pass so slowly

Yet so quickly and I begged for more time

It happens almost daily

One touch will prompt me

To stop me in my tracks

A hand on the small of my back

A kiss to my temple

Hands in my hair

A lingering kiss

A hug where we never wanted to let go

Take me back

Flashback

To a time when things were easy

Oh so smooth

I want it all back

Every sight

Of you approaching for an embrace

Each sound

Of you humming unaware

Your scent

I wish for it to last on my clothing

Your touch

I want it all

To flashback

To a time when things were easy

STARLIGHT

CONFESSION

I loved you

I always have

I always will

More than I care

To admit to you

I loved you when

You didn't love me

When you couldn't love me

When you shouldn't love me

But I loved you

From the beginning

Until now

Probably forevermore

Whether I like it or not

My love was given

My love was offered

Yours for the taking

Always accepted

I love you

I always have

I always will

My starlight confession

I will always love you

KING MIDAS HAS ASS'S EARS

MADELEINE MCDONALD

About the Author

Madeleine McDonald lives on the chilly east coast of England where the cliffs crumble into the sea. For many years she plundered family life to write newspaper columns and magazine articles. She listens to the radio while cooking or restoring furniture, and one of her radio stories was even translated into Mandarin Chinese and broadcast by the BBC World Service. Her travels have inspired romance novels set in Morocco and Switzerland. Her latest historical novel. A Shackled Inheritance, is set on a Caribbean sugar plantation in the time of the struggle to abolish slavery, and is available on Amazon.

What do you do in your leisure time?

I sew and garden

from

**Hornsea,
East Riding of
Yorkshire
England**

On the broad river of domestic calm

I drift, content

It was my choice

To seize upon a humdrum life

Husband and children

An endless ribbon of chores

Of mutual delights

And boundless rewards

In its place

You offered me the whirlwind

Insisting we would overcome challenges

Shoulder to shoulder

Hand in hand

A road so uncertain
I would not, could not follow

And yet

I whisper to the waving corn
And pray that you understand

King Midas has ass's ears
And I still love you too

END

- EFFORTS OF FRIENDSHIP
- ONE HOUR SHY OF ANOTHER

K. CARLTON JOHNSON

About the Author

My passion in life is to live the GOOD. To use everyday to it's fullest. I try to see each person in my day as gift. Poetry is the voice I use to speak to others of the joy of being human. Poetry, as all art, is a communication to others, a light to help us realize we are all connected.

What do you do in your leisure time?

I write poetry, assist at a local Hospice and care for an extended family.

EFFORTS OF

FRIENDSHIP

from

Lake Linden,
Michigan
U.S.A.

—————

Lift the barriers and let the light come in

Do not put away the tea cups, spoons, and silver,

celebrate the evening hours

the low moon and handy part of the wood

as it tips itself to pink

the gifts we brought were real, wrapped in tears, often

but joys as they approach the setting day washing back

are far more reliable than what we knew.

We have been considerate,

we have been harsh, but we needed to know

what the other wanted, so we forgave over and over.

Now, this light work of a passage narrowing

no more waste, we are simpler and looking

over the evening table, sip tea, as we watch

silver evening advance.

Quiet, so as to hear the last clouds song,

and conscious

That there are no walls between us.

ONE HOUR
SHY OF
ANOTHER

Holding hands

Turning towards the night

I do not know

What will happen

If you become real,

Maybe the world will collapse

Perhaps we will start,

 where we left off

Wet and exhausted from a vigorous swim

On a late summer evening.

- GRILLED CHEESE HOLD THE MEMORY
- RAN INTO ELVIS JESUS AND YOUR MEMORY AT WALMART
- MY THREE GRACES
- TOO GOOD FOR ME
- ONE WOMAN WATERFALL
- DOES HE
- I NEVER WRITE LOVE POEMS

JUDGE SANTIAGO BURDON

About the Author

On an unseasonably cool July morning in Chicago, equivalent to David Copperfield , Judge Burdon was born on a Friday. The Bronte Sisters, Keats, Burns and Dickens inspired his study of English Literature. He attended Universities in the United States, London and Paris directing his focus on Victorian novels and authors. His short stories and poems have been featured in; The Remnant Leaf, Stay Weird and Keep Writing, Independent Writer's Podcast, Spillwords, The Beatnik Cowboy, Down in the Dirt Magazine, The Raven Cage, Eskimo Pie, Across The Margin, Story Pub, Scarlet Leaf Review, Horror Sleaze Trash, The Stray Branch and Anti-Heroin Chic. Judge's first book "Stray Dogs and Deuces Wild Cautionary Tales" was published in January 2020 by HST PRESS. A book of Poetry "Not Real Poetry" is scheduled for release in May. He is presently engaged in finishing his Novel "Imitation of Myself." A non-fiction story encompassing his experiences as a drug runner for a Mexican Cartel. Judge celebrated his 67th birthday last July and lives modestly in Costa Rica.

GRILLED CHEESE

HOLD THE MEMORY

from

San Jose, Costa Rica

If I only knew what you were thinking
I'd feel warmer against the cold
Than with my coat
Avoiding the words I've heard
Crying out to be spoken
Regretting the letters I never wrote
It's been quite awhile since I've seen you last
How the years they've passed us by
The tears we've cried have long been dried
Things have changed they always do
We're different now doesn't matter anyhow
Tell me how you've been
Still with the warm smile I see
Hope that smile is for me
I've been living out west in Tucson
Ya know fun in the sun
Just getting by but not by much
No bad times I still don't have
a dime to my name
Chicago hasn't changed it still seems the same
You say they had a lot of snow in Wisconsin

It gets oh so cold and the wind it blows so damn hard
I'm still smoking and playing guitar
But I'm not getting far
So tell me did you find that special someone
you'd make sure would be nothing like me
Or is he still a mystery
I know I made a mess of love
Like dirt I swept it under the rug
To be forgotten
Thanks for the great grilled cheese
Oh how we survived on these
Every time I eat one it brings back fond memories
Of you know back then
Another cup of coffee then I've got to run
That's such a good line especially at this time
Don't say we'll keep in touch or how much
you've missed me
I just stopped by for your famous grilled cheese
And a broken memory that can never be.......

RAN INTO
ELVIS JESUS
AND YOUR
MEMORY AT
WALMART

Left toothbrushless mine pilfered along with shampoo, deodorant, razors and other such, found me wasted in Walmart, thieving Gnomes at the last homeless shelter are my suspects. His name tag said Elvis, greeting customers at the starting gate, navigating shopping cart jockeys with cherubs riding shotgun, my request for the location of items is answered Presley style "Past houseware" he Hound Dogged lip curled.

Among waffle irons and toasters in an aisle devoid of housewife print skirts, your memory purchased my thoughts, forging past bedding, linen sheets how we once tangled and ravaged, is that your image disappearing into lingerie.

Jesus on his employee name badge suffering from price tag neurosis. "Love potion? We don't sell that vagabundo polo." He growled with picante breath.

You told me I could find everything I needed here, but not even Walmart has what it would take to make you love me again.

I hope Target is open!

MY THREE

GRACES

Agalia
arizona goddess blossom of society's elite
living your mother's dreams and wishes.
scottsdale pretty boys.

Thalia
vail heiress
your wealth cultivated from
beans and canned corn condominium queen

Euphorsyne
santa barbara debutante
daddy's money choking your freedom.
b.m.w. mentality
calculated bad girl.

I'm beer and stale cigarettes
not cognac and cigars
it's your world
with checkbooks balanced
paris holidays
matching bras and panties
your questions never go unanswered.

my world
sweat stained collar
southside of chicago
worn like a tattoo
exposed in my speech
dago kid with coarse demeanor
public schools
vagrant morals
empty pockets

yet you take me in like a stray puppy.
you name after bronte's heathcliff
I bark poetry
scratch words of love
I howl romance
you give me
groomed pussy
airplane tickets
and dead presidents
in return for orgasms
rendered as restitution
without receipts
a gift with the price tag unremoved

you make love to me in pity
I tongue your trigger in triumph
holes in my socks amuse you
tan lines and lipstick shades your life's concerns
my existence paid for with humility
yours with credit cards never overextended
balances rising
long distance phone lines crackle
more empty promises.

TOO GOOD

FOR ME

You want me to be a dancer but my rhythm is in my speech, you're always asking me for answers, when the words are out of reach.
you say I've got no angel, watching over me, she left to be a hooker, turning tricks out in the street.
You think I should step careful, and not talk so loud, you say I'm hard to handle, I lend no comfort in a crowd.
Look at you, standing naked in the rain, You praying for lovers that never came, You can't dream beyond your pain. You, you're too good for me.

I live without direction, my compass is the breeze, my mirror with no reflection, my song has no melody.
The bottle feeds my madness, my denial cures the pain, my storm lends only thunder, never brings the healing rain, you say I'm wild and restless, I live life for the now, my Genie granted a death wish,I'm more than the law will allow.
Look at you a toxic valentine.
You your dozen not worth a dime. You, your poetry always rhymes
You you're too good for me

Time is such a skilled thief
Steals what we never know is gone, There's no future in a tea leaf,
Always sacrifice your pawn
My handshake hides a clenched fist, My smile disguises my
disdain, My love breeds an infection, No cure for the disease and
pain

You, your candle burnt out long ago You always doing what you're
told You your promise bought and sold.

You, you're too good for me.

ONE WOMAN WATERFALL

On guard

Weapons drawn

Razor edged dialogue

Cutting deep into the last breath of affection

Words spewing like acid,

staining our masterpiece.

Colors melting into gray

bubbling with the sounds of disaster

"Fuck You's" crescendo

into the odor of hate

Your Teflon tongue spills explanations

with non stick sincerity

A reservoir of "I'm sorrys"

burst into a flood of tears

You become a one woman waterfall

Your love was financed

Compounding interest

Loan shark terms

With a heart that carried a second mortgage

I'm the victim of foreclosure

Left empty, blindsided, cold cocked

From your drive by lie

Our love now crippled and maimed

Searching for a handicapped parking place

DOES HE

Does he touch you with deep cabernet dreams

or is it all white wine passion

does your heart race from his nearness

is there surrender in his scent

does he tempt you

does he leave you breathless

are you tantalized with jalapeno kisses

like butterflies stinging spicy pleasure on your inner thighs

does he entice you

do you feel wicked and waxened

do you scream bruja's incantations

moan verses of ancient runes

is your orgasm seismic

does he read like a mystery with a hint of gypsy blood

does he consume you

can he make you laugh in color

does he feed your madness calm your storm

does he feel betrayed by your shadow

is he envious and jealous of your light

does he sit in stillness while you listen to your muse

does he make you feel whole

does he

does he

I once did

didn't I

I NEVER WRITE LOVE POEMS

You say I never write love poems.

It doesn't mean I don't feel that way.

With all the love you've shown me

You are my reason to live every day.

When we're lieing holding each other

We feel the moment

We don't need the words.

You say I never write love poems.

I know you've given me reason to.

It's not that I'm uninspired

There's just no poem that comes close to you.

When you kiss me it's such a feeling,

Words can't express

What you do to me.

You say I never write love poems,

Declaring my desire for you.

You are my living poem

A breathing Sonnet

I'm just a sentence lost within a verse.

My pen is idle while my heart beats in rhythm

To the sound of your voice

Like the melody of a song

You say I never write love poems

I plead you forgive my indigent hand

Empty of words to create a love poem

Filled with the emotion of a Cupid's scribe.

After all the love we've shared together

You can read the story

Written in my smile

Someday the words

They may come easy.

In the whisper of a gentle breeze.

Until then I live with the sin

Of the love poem my soul has kept hidden

Your love poem

The one,

That has never been written

US

KATHERINE ABRAHAM

About the Author

Katherine Abraham is the Author of Yesterday Once More, Silenced by Love and Some Days are Forever. An Adventist, and the grand-daughter of a missionary, Katherine is a teacher by profession, who has studied Law, Literature and Journalism. She writes poetry and prose for various online publications as well as International Anthologies. She recently worked as a researcher for Dr. Shashi Tharoor's latest book, The Battle of Belonging(2021). She is also the host for a New International Podcast Series for Christians entitled, Chasing Hope where she talks of Christians and the various aspects of a principled Christian life.

Website : www.chasinghopewithkatherine.com

Author's website: www.katherinerabraham.com

Her fourth novel "Every Sunset Has a Story" is now with the publishers.

The Rice Bag's Argument is her first attempt at non-fiction chronicling the efforts of the Christians in the pre Independence, Freedom Struggle and post Independence periods. The book seeks to set some records straight.

What do you do in your leisure time?

Katherine indulges in a plethora of activities in her leisure time. She is keen on wildlife and landscape photography, loves to sketch and is currently learning oil painting. She also works for various causes and partners with different NGOs from time to time. She is currently working on helping a youth initiative seeking to help young people how to refine their Spoken English Skills.

from

Pune, India

Destiny may never bring us together

Time may tear us apart

We have too many thoughts of tomorrow

Why not spend a little thought on the magic of today's love- craft?

We thought of tomorrow

Thinking we have one

Destiny believes it knows better

We know now we have none.

Fate called up this morning

Beguiling me to choose another

"Why should I?"

I listen carefully

"You're too young," he says

"Your life will be a waste

if you make this decision in haste."

In the silence of my thoughts
I would much rather be chaste.

Have you ever loved someone
Made promises to be together
Always and forever?
Love happens once
Now solitude will be my partner.

We are partners in crime
A crime so pure and true
It is beautiful how even in our thoughts
The first words that bind us together are
"I love you…"

A mist of uncertainty now surrounds us
Don't think any more my love
For there will come a day
When we will be blessed
And You and I will sit
At the end of another rainbow
Snuggled in a blanket of love
Then it will be us
Us and no other
Us together, never to part…

THE INCIDENT ON HOWRAH BRIDGE

RATING **(MATURE, PARANORMAL)**

NOEL LORENZ

What do you do in
your leisure time?

I write poetry,
assist writers
publish their
works, plot short
stories, take
interviews, host
open-mics and
review poems.
I live in the
present moment.

About the Author

An author and a publisher from the city of joy, Kolkata, India. A Zen practitioner since 2013.

My grandfather has been my inspiration and later on, I got motivated by reading Rabindranath Tagore, Gulzar, Shakespeare, George Bernard Shaw, William Wordsworth, Leo Tolstoy, Paulo Coelho, Robert Ludlum and Nora Roberts.

Publishing was my dream and today, with the help of writers from India and around the globe and graces of god, I am a publisher. This would be incomplete if I do not mention two names. I am grateful to my mother for supporting and motivting me althrough and the Brand Ambassadors of The Indian & World Literature Series from my publishing house, Noel Lorenz House of Fiction.

www.noellorenz.com

Instagram/Twitter/Facebook @noellorenzbooks

'Zen Mind' is the first non-fiction that I have released. Planning another soon.

CHAPTER 1
SUICIDE

from

She wore a red pajama and headed for the clinic. It was a cold late December night. Everyone was busy in prepping for the new year, and here she was, worried to her toes and trembled as she entered the clinic.

Sakshi, as she was known in her friend circle, made her way to the doctor's chamber.

An hour later, on the Howrah Bridge, people were gathered near the railings trying to take a look below where the search and rescue operation was on.

A woman had jumped in to the dark Ganges river at 8.30 pm local time. A person standing near had seen her wearing a red pajama and he informed the local police that she stood there all the time he walked toward her from the other end of the bridge. He didn't see her face as she faced the river all this time. He was shocked when she climbed up the railing. He couldn't believe his eyes and wiped it to make sure he was not dreaming. By then, she was off the edge and his eyes could only follow her trail.

CHAPTER 2
BACK AT HOME

9.30 PM

Sakshi, "Hey Rahul! Please taste this. I made it specially for you."

"Oh, no, no. No more please. I already had enough."

Meenakshi smiled sitting beside Rahul, "You can't say no." She looked up at Sakshi and added, "Hey, give him some." The girls laughed as Rahul was fed.

"Okay, now while I am having this, you've gotta tell us about Suresh."

"Can I tell you later?"

"Ofcourse not. We wanna hear it now." Meenakshi added.

They looked at Sakhshi who became a little serious.

"Well, I have found no way out and I am confused."

"About?" Rahul asked, worried.

"I'm pregnant.

Rahul and Meenakshi eyed each other.

"And his family is not ready to accept me as I am from a different cast."

"Oh, these higher caste people!" Meenakshi exclaimed.

"Actually, I am the higher caste here. They had a death in their family when married outside their caste so they are worried about their son."

"And what about you?" Rahul asked.

"I will tell you tomorrow," Sakshi smiled.

After the dinner Rahul and Meenakshi said their goodbyes and left for home.

CHAPTER 3
NEXT MORNING

6.50 AM

"Hey, Meenu. Come here, now."

Hearing a worried call from Rahul, Meenakshi ran to the living room.

"Yesterday we left Sakhshi's apartment at 10.25, didn't we?"

"Yes, why are asking now?"

"Look," he pointed toward the television.

Meenakshi turned to watch the television. The news channel was on. Sakshi's face was displayed and the news read:

'A woman in her late twenties jumped off the Howrah Bridge at 8.30PM on Saturday. The body was recovered at 10PM and identified as Sakshi Singh from the Salt Lake neighborhood.'

THE END

WWW.NOELLORENZ.COM
WWW.NOELLORENZ.COM/RADIO